D0482082

Hook Moon Night

Hook Moon Night

SPOOKY TALES FROM THE GEORGIA MOUNTAINS

Faye Gibbons
illustrated by Ronald Himler

Morrow Junior Books
New York

To Miriam Rinn,
my talented first editor and
treasured friend

Text copyright © 1997 by Faye Gibbons
Illustrations copyright © 1997 by Ronald Himler

Published by Morrow Junior Books
a division of William Morrow and Company, Inc.
1350 Avenue of the Americas, New York, NY 10019

Printed in the United States of America.

3 4 5 6 7 8 9 10

Library of Congress Cataloging-in-Publication Data
Gibbons, Faye.
Hook moon night: spooky tales from the Georgia Mountains / by Faye Gibbons.
p. cm.
Summary: A collection of seven hair-raising yarns, told one night on a mountain porch in Georgia.
ISBN 0-688-14504-3
1. Mountain life—Georgia—Juvenile fiction.   2. Georgia—Juvenile fiction.   3. Horror tales, American.
4. Children's stories, American.   [1. Mountain life—Georgia—Fiction.   2. Georgia—Fiction.   3. Horror
stories.   4. Short stories.]   I. Title.
PZ7.G33913N1 1997   [Fic]—dc21   96-37745   CIP AC

Contents

Author's Note

Carter's Quarter, Georgia. You won't find Carter's Quarter on any map, but it's a real place—or used to be. Named for a long-ago Sam Carter, who was said to have owned a quarter of a million acres, the land ranges from hilly to mountainous, and most of it is stony. My father used to say that it would take a quarter of a million acres to make a living. And he should know, because he and his eight brothers and sisters helped my grandparents wring a bare living from 120 acres of that land. My father's people were tough, self-sufficient, and thrifty. Though most of them had little formal education, they were intelligent people who never forgot anything—especially a good story.

They told those stories at family gatherings. During front-porch weather—from spring through much of autumn—my mill worker parents, my three brothers, my sister, and I frequently visited the homes of various country relatives on weekends. The adults claimed the rockers and cane-bottomed chairs, and we young'uns lay on the splintered porches or sat on the steps to listen to the stories of family history, the hunting yarns, even the stories with lessons at the end. But as the day wore on and darkness moved in, the scary stories would begin—tales of ghosts, or "haints," as my country relatives called them, and stories of premonitions and unexplained deaths.

I drew on those hair-raising yarns for the stories offered here. Imagine yourself on a dark porch many miles from the nearest electric lights and indoor plumbing. Listen to the night sounds and the storytellers.

ON THE PORCH

A silver hook of a moon hung over the corncrib when Mike Nolan settled down on the porch next to his grandfather's rocker. It was very dark, and the early July heat had dwindled to a pleasant level. Other than that from stars and fireflies, the only light was the flickering yellow glow from a kerosene lamp in the kitchen, where some of the womenfolk were finishing supper dishes.

This farm gave Mike the creeps. Even in daylight, before his parents had dropped him off and left, he hadn't liked the looks of the place. It was so much wilder and more run-down than the last time he'd seen it four years ago. The unpainted house and outbuildings were still the same ghostly gray, but the chimneys seemed to lean more to one side. The woods were closer, too. Marching across the abandoned fields, half-grown pines surrounded the house on all sides. It was if they were trying to run the people out, Mike thought.

Mike had wanted to tell his parents how he felt, but how could he when his younger brother and sister were right there, listening to every word he said? Ernie and Kate had cried a little when their mother and father drove off, but Mike was twelve. He had managed to put up a good front when his father called, "See you next week, kids. We'll have a house and jobs by then."

The light in the kitchen finally went out, and the women came and took the last rockers and cane-bottomed chairs. The children who had been sitting in them shoved in next to Mike, Ernie, Kate, and the other cousins on the splintery porch floor.

"Reckon we're going to have to be going before too long," drawled Uncle Cecil. He'd said that several times already but had made no move toward his truck yet.

"Yeah, I guess we could be heading home ourselves," said Uncle John Ed.

No danger of that, thought Mike.

A sudden shrieking sound cut through the darkness. "What was that?" asked one of the cousins.

"Sh-h-h-h-h!" said one of the adults.

A shiver prickled Mike's neck. Now he heard nothing more than the usual night sounds of this place—the chirp of crickets, the call of a whippoorwill, the chorus of bullfrogs down at the spring. They were the same sounds he'd heard a short while before, when he had taken the jug of milk to the spring to cool. The noises had seemed harmless enough then. Now they seemed threatening.

"Sounded like it was coming from the graves up on the hill," another cousin suggested.

Mike knew which graves he meant. Just this afternoon the same cousin had shown him the sunken hollows where their great-great-grandparents were buried.

"Reckon it's a haint?" asked one of the older Nolan cousins.

"No, it ain't no spirit," said Grandma Nolan. "It was more'n likely a rabbit that got caught by an owl."

Grandpa Nolan stirred in his rocker. "Might be. But on the other hand, them Nolans buried on the hill died back when folks around Carter's Quarter didn't use doctors or undertakers. Back then, neighbors took care of such things. A local man would build a pine coffin, and some woman in the neighborhood would lay the body out. Then they had the funeral."

"Don't start on them scary tales, Floyd," said Grandma Nolan.

There was a pause, and for a moment Mike thought that was the end of it. Then Grandpa went on, his voice dropping lower, "Likely a lot of folks back then got buried *alive*."

"Buried alive?" said Mike. The very thought terrified him.

"I know the women that laid out dead folks tried to be careful," Grandpa continued. "But it stands to reason sometimes they *thought* a feller was dead when maybe he was still alive."

"Well," said Uncle Cecil from the end of the porch, "in a case like that, I don't reckon a feller stayed alive *long*."

Mike laughed along with everyone else on the porch, but it was nervous laughter.

"That's so," Grandpa replied when the laughter had died down, "but on a night like tonight strange things can happen."

"What do you mean, a night like tonight?" asked one of the girl cousins.

Grandpa let the question hang there in the darkness for just a moment before answering. "They say, when a hook moon like this'un shines on a new grave where the body's resting uneasy, that person's spirit can come out to make trouble."

"Floyd, you stop scaring the young'uns," said Grandma.

Grandpa went right on. "Now, I don't know for a certain fact that all they told is so, but some folks back when I was growing up'd swear to it. Especially in the case of that Siler woman over beyond Bell Mountain. They say there was just this kind of moon the night after she was buried...."

THE BURIAL

S he can't be dead," said Amy Harkins, looking at the woman on the bed. "People don't die from chills and fever! Granny Turpin sent me to sit up with Miz Siler and give her medicine. Granny didn't say nothing about dying."

Shirley Wilbanks threw herself on the bed, crying. "Mama, Mama! Don't die! Come back!"

Amy felt tears stinging her own eyes, but Delvin Wilbanks pushed his wife aside, leaned over the still form of his mother-in-law, and removed her earrings. "I'll just take these earbobs and wedding ring for safekeeping," he said after a moment.

"Don't," said Shirley. "Please don't take

Mama's jewelry, Delvin. They ain't worth that much. I want to bury her in them." She looked imploringly at Amy, but the girl felt helpless. She wasn't even a member of the family. She was just a fifteen-year-old sent by her grandmother to sit up with a sick neighbor.

"Earbobs and a gold band ain't going to do your mama no good in the ground," said Delvin Wilbanks, slipping them into his pocket. "She can't take her jewels, her money, or her land where she's gone. That all belongs to me now." He reached for a purse on the table next to the bed.

Shirley grabbed for his hand. "Don't go through Mama's pocketbook, Delvin. It ain't the time."

Delvin shoved the purse under his arm. "You're right," he said. "We got to get her outta this bed. It's hard to get a body straight if you wait till it gets stiff." He turned to his nearly grown sons standing in the doorway. "Gus, Billy—fetch them two benches from the kitchen and put 'em side by side over next to the wall."

"Wait," said Amy. "First get me a looking glass!" She'd suddenly remembered what her grandmother always did to make sure a person was dead before preparing the body for burial. Maybe, oh, maybe...

She snatched the mirror that one of the

Wilbanks girls handed her and polished it on her apron. While the family waited, she held it to the woman's mouth, then her nose.

"Please let the glass fog up," she prayed softly, but the mirror stayed clear. Putting her ear against the woman's chest, she listened. There was no heartbeat. Finally, she picked up the slender hand and checked for a pulse in the wrist. Again nothing.

"All right, I guess you can put her on the benches," Amy finally told Delvin Wilbanks, "and then send one of your boys after my granny."

"Why in the land would I want to do that?" he asked.

"Granny's the one that lays out dead folks. I only help her sometimes."

"It'd be dark by the time a person could get to her place!" he said.

Amy looked out the window and was surprised to see how low the sun had gotten. Delvin Wilbanks was right—it was a good seven miles to Granny Turpin's. "Well, send for her anyway," she said. "If you send somebody tonight, she can come here first thing in the morning."

Delvin grunted with impatience. "Why can't you lay her out?"

"I will," said Amy, acting braver than she felt. "But I still need Granny Turpin here to make sure everything's done right."

He nodded reluctantly. "Well, all right. Gus, you leave soon as we get her on these benches and, Billy, you go tell Joe Dodson that we need a coffin right now. Then go on to the preacher's house and tell him we'll need him to say a few words over her tomorrow."

"Tomorrow?" said Amy, surprised. It seemed a little soon, but then it was June and you couldn't keep a body out too long in warm weather.

Word traveled fast. By the time Amy had bathed and dressed the body, the nearest neighbor had arrived, bringing food and promising more for the next day. The woman's friendliness wasn't the unreserved kind Amy usually saw when a death occurred in a family. She had few words for Delvin. Her smiles were all for his wife. None of the neighbors liked Delvin Wilbanks, but they had liked Betty Siler and they felt sorry for her only child, Shirley.

Two more women arrived as Amy combed Betty Siler's hair. "I'd do anything for Betty," said Bee Dodson when Shirley tried to thank her. "Joe'll have the coffin here early in the morning, and the Petty boys said they'd dig the grave."

The women inspected the body and nodded approvingly. "Don't she look natural?" one said.

"I've never seen a dead person with that much color in the face," another said.

Amy swung around to look at Betty Siler again. The woman *did* have color in her face—far too much color for a dead person. Amy picked up the wrist once more. Still nothing. A short while later, when the women had gone, Amy discovered something even more unsettling. When she was straightening Betty Siler's dress, she found that the woman was still warm under the arms. How could that be? Well, Granny Turpin would take over in the morning, and she would know what was to be done.

It was getting on toward midday by the time Gus Wilbanks returned. He was alone. "Miz Turpin's with Edgar Childers's baby," he told Amy. "Your grandpaw said the young'un was real bad off and you'd just have to make out the best you could."

"But I can't," Amy cried. "Granny's got to come and check Miz Siler." Amy looked around at the neighbor women who'd come to bring food and pay their last respects. Some of them were doing housecleaning chores, but all of them were listening to everything that went on. Amy motioned for Delvin and Shirley Wilbanks to step into Betty Siler's room and then closed the door.

"Miz Siler's *still* warm under the arms this morning," she told them.

Shirley Wilbanks's face lit up. "Glory be! You mean maybe..."

Delvin Wilbanks grunted. "What do you expect? It's June." Shirley's face fell. "We can't just set down and wait for your granny to take a notion to come over."

"Well, send for a doctor, then," Amy said.

"What! That'd cost a fortune, and it'd take another day or more. Besides, it's a waste of time. No doctor I know of can bring dead people back to life. We're having the funeral *today*."

"Then give me time to go talk to Granny," Amy begged. "Let me ask her about this. Let me be sure."

"Delvin, please," said Shirley. "Do this one

thing for me, and I'll not say no more about the wedding band and the earbobs. You can have 'em."

Delvin scowled at the body still stretched out on the benches. "It's a waste of time. We can't wait forever. She's going to be stinking."

Amy tried one last time. "Just think how it'd be to wake up in the cold and dark, buried forever."

Shirley broke into sobs.

"How fast can you get there and back?" Delvin asked.

"Fast," said Amy. "Real fast. I'm a good runner." Even as she said it, she thought of the return trip. It would include her grandmother, who couldn't run at all.

"Well, if you hurry..."

Amy grabbed him by the hand. "Thank you, Mr. Wilbanks. I'll hurry fast as I can."

Amy ran for the first mile or more. But then her side began to hurt, and she had to slow to a fast walk. She took every shortcut she knew of between the Siler homeplace and the Childers house, but still the sun got higher and higher in the sky. Then it was noon and afternoon. It was midafternoon by the time the Childers house came into view. Amy found a new spurt of energy and ran all the way. She burst in through the open doorway without even knocking.

"Amy!" said Granny Turpin, who was sitting in a rocker with the baby. "What in tarnation is the matter?"

"Miz Siler," Amy gasped. "Under her arms...she's warm."

"Get your breath, child," said her grand-mother.

"And have a drink of water," said Eva Childers, hurrying to her with the dipper and water bucket.

Amy gulped down two dippers full of the fresh, cold water and then began again. "Miz Siler's dead."

Granny Turpin's eyes grew large. "Ah! I figured her to pull out of this."

"I checked just like you do for breath and a heartbeat."

Granny Turpin nodded. "Good." She took the baby to the bed and laid it between two pillows and then spread a lace curtain over it to keep flies from bothering it.

"But, Granny, she ain't cold under the arms!"

Granny Turpin turned, her eyes narrowed. "Ain't cold? When did she die?"

"Yesterday evening, getting on to sundown. And that ain't all. Her color ain't right. She ain't pale like a dead person's supposed to be. And Delvin Wilbanks is wanting to go ahead and bury her anyway. I begged and begged him to wait for you, and he finally give in and let me come fetch you."

Granny's mouth became a tight line. She turned to Mrs. Childers. "I have to go. The baby's going to be all right, now that his fever's broke."

While Granny Turpin gathered her medicines and loaded them into her satchel, Eva Childers dropped pieces of corn bread into a flour sack. Granny took the sack and gave the satchel to Amy.

Amy was dismayed at the weight of it. "Granny, we got to hurry. Can't we leave this?"

Granny shook her head. "I never know what I might need." Turning back to Eva Childers, she said, "When your man gets in from the fields, tell him I may want him over at the Siler homeplace. Delvin Wilbanks might require a little help making up his mind to do the right thing."

The sun sank lower and lower in the sky as Amy and her granny headed back to the Siler place. Hard as they tried, it was dusk when they saw the house up ahead. Shirley Wilbanks was on the porch when they arrived, sitting in a rocker.

Amy waved. "I'm back, Miz Wilbanks. And I got Granny. She's going to check your mama."

Shirley Wilbanks dropped her face into her hands and broke into sobs.

"We already had the funeral," said Delvin Wilbanks from the doorway.

Stunned, Amy stared at him. "But you promised."

"I didn't do any such thing, if you think back on it. I said enough to hush you up. We done what we had to do, and now it's over. Old lady Siler had her way when she was alive. Now I'm getting what's mine. Like I said, it's over."

"No, it ain't over," said Granny Turpin. "We're going to dig her up and check on her right now."

Delvin laughed. "I don't see how an old lady and a skinny little gal can do much digging. Besides, it's near on two miles from here to the burying ground at the church. It'll be full dark by the time you get there. And they ain't hardly no moon tonight."

Amy looked up. The moon was only a skinny crescent in a darkening sky. Delvin was right. They couldn't do it tonight.

"Then we'll have to spend the night with you and go first thing in the morning," said Granny Turpin. "It may be too late, but we have to check. As for the digging, I got help coming for that."

"Help? You gossiping old fool. Have you been making trouble for me with the neighbors?"

"You don't need no help on that," Granny Turpin told him.

Grudgingly, Delvin allowed them to sleep in Betty Siler's room. It wasn't where Amy wanted to pass the night, but she could do it with her grandmother's company.

Sometime in the night Amy was jolted from a deep sleep by what sounded like the bellow of a wild animal. She sat upright in bed. "Wh-wh-what!" she said.

"Sh-h-h-h-h!" said her grandmother.

Amy listened. The bellowing had turned into crazy jabbering. The only words Amy could understand were "Let me out! Let me outta here!" It was the voice of Delvin Wilbanks. Then there was the voice of Shirley. She sounded consoling. Finally, there was quiet.

It seemed to Amy she had hardly gotten back to sleep when the bellowing came again. This time there were also heavy footsteps in the hallway and then talking. All night it continued: periods of uneasy quiet followed by bursts of crying and pacing.

When Amy and Granny Turpin stepped out of their room the next morning, Delvin Wilbanks was waiting for them. He had dark circles under his eyes. "I'll dig for you," he said.

"Let's go, then," said Granny.

Carrying a shovel in one hand and a hoe in the other, Delvin nearly ran the two miles to the church. Granny fell behind, but Amy stayed right with him. Delvin didn't bother to remove the jars of flowers neighbors had placed on the mounded-up dirt. He just kicked them aside and fell to digging. Throwing dirt in every direction, he paid no attention as his wife and children arrived. Nor did he seem to notice when Jim Shaw and several other men circled around.

Going at it like a crazy man, Delvin dug himself deeper and deeper into the grave. His face was soon glistening with sweat, but he did not rest, and he refused polite offers of help from a couple of the men. Amy wondered how he could keep going. But he did, and at last there came a dull thud of metal scraping against wood. The crowd gathered closer and watched Delvin expose the coffin lid.

"Help me out of here," Delvin said, tossing up his shovel. Taking the hand of the nearest man, he scrambled out and grabbed his hoe.

A murmur ran through the group as Delvin reached down and hooked the casket lid with the hoe. With a creaking sound, the cover slowly lifted.

"Oh, no!" he screamed. "It's the way I seen her last night, only I was in there with her." Shirley Wilbanks screamed and fell to the ground.

Amy didn't want to look, but she had to.

Betty Siler's eyes and mouth were open. Her hands clutched tatters of the coffin lining. She no longer had the color in her face that had been so worrisome yesterday. Now she was as pale as death.

Granny Turpin heaved a great sigh. "Close the lid and fill in the grave," she said to Jim Shaw. "It's too late now."

Turning to Delvin Wilbanks, she said, "For one time you're right. I think you're just beginning to get what's yours."

C

"Did Betty Siler settle down after that?" asked Mike. "Or did she keep on haunting Delvin Wilbanks?"

"Nobody knows exactly what happened," said Grandpa. "Delvin disappeared a few days after he dug up his mother-in-law."

"Reckon he was in that coffin with Miz Siler?" asked one of the cousins.

"Could be," Grandpa replied. "And they thought of that. But nobody wanted to dig up that grave again to find out."

"I wouldn't ever dig up a grave," said Mike.

"Me neither," said Ernie and Kate together.

"Digging up a grave is a serious thing," Grandpa agreed.

"Remember when the government was sending in all them men to dig up Indian graves a few years ago?" said a voice Mike recognized as Aunt Dorrie's. "Course, it was *old* graves."

Grandma grunted in disapproval. "Don't matter. They had no business disturbing the dead."

"You're right about that, Ora," said Grandpa. "That reminds me of the story about how the Caudill boy dug up that Indian over next to the river. Yes sir, Joel Caudill was looking for riches, but what he found was something he didn't want a'tall...."

THE INDIAN GHOST

Digging up an Indian grave from hundreds of years ago ain't the same as digging up regular graves," Joel told his cousin Tom. "I already told you that a dozen times."

Stubbornly, Tom refused the shovel Joel was urging on him and put a new worm on his hook. "A grave's a grave," he said, and dropped his line back in the river. He hadn't caught a thing, but he kept up the pretense that he was fishing.

"You're going to be sorry," Joel said, making one last attempt. He'd already dug in four places along the riverbank, and he was getting tired. "When I find a treasure, you're going to be real sorry."

Unmoved, Tom propped himself against a willow. "Maybe you'll be the one that's sorry."

Joel could see he was beat. He leaned on his shovel and looked downstream. "Let's see," he whispered. "Uncle John Henry said the grave was in line with the bluff and that tall oak upstream, and right even with that big rock over there."

Just as Joel marked an X on the ground with his foot, he heard the howl of a dog. It was a mournful wail that rose and fell and then blended into the sounds of the wind and the river.

Joel shivered. "Wonder what's wrong with that dog."

"What dog?" Tom asked.

Joel frowned and then shrugged. Maybe it had just been the wind.

He checked his sightings again and pushed his shovel into the dirt. Lucky for him, the soil in this spot was sandy instead of the clay that was common along the river. "That grave's gotta be right here," he said to his cousin. "Uncle John Henry said..."

"I know—he found a grave and saw an Indian with a neckpiece and armbands on him," Tom said, finishing up the tale their uncle had told them several days before. "That's been twenty-five years. Maybe the river changed its banks. A flood could've washed the bones away. Or maybe somebody else found the grave. People've gone crazy since those men started coming in and digging up Indian stuff."

"That's true," Joel admitted. The men had been asking local people about the best places to dig, and they'd offered money for the information. In fact, that's what had set Joel on fire. If they'd offer five dollars for a good digging location, how much might they give for Indian jewelry already dug up?

Joel kept digging. "The grave's here," he said. "Maybe a whole bunch of graves. And I'm gonna get rich."

"More likely you're gonna get wet," said Tom, pulling in his line. "It's about to rain."

Joel glanced at the darkening sky and dug faster. Another rain was all he needed! That would finish out the whole rotten week. His parents and Tom's had sent them to help their elderly uncle and aunt gather crops and cut wood for the coming winter. It had already rained twice, and between the weather and the chores, this had been their first chance to come to the river. And tomorrow they were going home.

Suddenly Joel's shovel struck something. The howl sounded again, but this time he scarcely heard it. Squatting, he dug with his bare hands.

"What'd you find?" asked Tom, taking a few steps toward him.

"I don't know," said Joel. "Could be a pot." It was something round and hard.

Slinging dirt right and left, he dug faster. Impatient, he grabbed the thing with both hands and tugged. Not until it broke loose did he realize what he held. A skull. The empty eye sockets stared up at him as though they saw right through him.

Joel yelped and fell backward. Seemingly with a life of its own, the skull popped out of his hands and tumbled over and over until it came to rest against a clump of dead grass. It lay right side up, looking at him. For an endless moment, Joel's gaze was locked on the eyeless sockets.

The howl came again and seemed to vibrate through his body.

"Tarnation," said Tom. "Hadn't you better put that back?"

Joel jumped up and shook himself. "I'll do that later, when I fill in the hole," he said, and used his foot to turn the skull facedown in the dirt.

Tom frowned and shook his head, but Joel ignored him. Tom stood at a distance as Joel returned to digging. But he edged nearer when his cousin began uncovering what had to be the ribs of the Indian.

Then Joel saw a disklike piece of metal with designs etched into its surface. As his hand closed around it, it seemed to grow warm under his touch.

"Let's go," said Tom, backing up.

"Wait," said Joel. "Hand me that burlap bag."

Tom hesitated a moment and then kicked the bag toward his cousin. He watched, scowling, as Joel placed the disk into the bag.

Minutes later Joel found armbands and resisted the temptation to try them on. Then he found dozens of beads.

Tom picked up the fishing poles. "I'm going."

"I'm not finished," Joel said, but a fine mist was moving in, driven by a wind growing steadily stronger. The overcast sky had become darker, and the light had taken on a strange greenish cast. Then he looked at the skull. It was upright, and the eye sockets looked right at him once more. The wind did it, he told himself. But still, he was ready to leave.

"Just give me time to fill in this hole," he said, but Tom continued to edge away from the riverbank. Joel shoveled in the grave hurriedly and patted down the dirt. Tom kept retreating, but he was going slowly, so Joel caught up with him at the far edge of the pasture, near their uncle's mailbox.

"Rain won't hurt this Indian stuff," Joel said, setting the burlap bag down by the mailbox, behind a clump of blackberry vines. "So I'll leave it here till I head home tomorrow."

"Good," said Tom, who was already on the road.

Joel ran to catch up and then stopped, listening. "No fooling, Tom, don't you hear that dog?"

Tom looked at him for a moment before shaking his head. "I don't hear a thing. Let's go."

It was nearly dark, and the mist had become a hard, sleety rain by the time the boys got to their aunt and uncle's house. Aunt Lucy was doddering about the kitchen, heating leftover turnip greens, corn bread, and potatoes. Uncle

John Henry was finishing the chair bottom he'd been caning for days.

"You boys been gone long enough," said their aunt. "Catch any fish?"

"No'm," answered Joel.

"Tried to tell you ain't no fish biting today," said John Henry. "You got wet for nothing."

It was fully dark by the time they sat down to eat. Whipped by a cold draft, the flame of the kerosene lamp cast a ghostly light around the kitchen. Eerie shadows crept over the wall. The rain pinged against the windows and drummed on the metal roof. And every now and then Joel heard the howl. It seemed louder and more distinct each time.

There was another sound, too—a sound Joel couldn't make out and sometimes wasn't sure he heard. He watched the others around the table, hoping someone else would notice. Once he thought John Henry heard. The old man cocked his head as though listening. "Mean rain," he finally said.

"The river'll be up," Lucy added.

"Puts me in mind of the big rain we had after I found the Indian grave that time," John Henry said.

Joel felt a chill. He swallowed hard. From the corner of his eye, he saw Tom look at him, but he evaded his cousin's gaze.

"About this time of year, it was," John Henry

continued, leaning across the table. "Did I ever tell you boys about the time I found the Indian grave betwixt the bluff and the oak tree?"

Both boys nodded, but John Henry went right on. "I was walking fencerows like I did every fall, seeing where repair was needed. When I got to the far side of the river pasture, I seen something that made ever hair on my neck stand up."

"An Indian skeleton," said Joel, wanting to hurry the scary tale to its conclusion.

"An Indian skeleton," said John Henry, just as if Joel hadn't spoken. "I guess rain had washed the dirt off it. Anyway, it was laid out there with the skull looking at me like it could see me."

Joel knew exactly what his uncle meant. He remembered in spite of himself that skull and those empty eye sockets.

John Henry wiped a bony hand over his mouth. "The Indian had jewelry on. Neckpieces, armbands, and suchlike."

Joel swallowed hard. "Did you—did you keep anything?"

John Henry's watery eyes grew large. "Lord, no! You think I'm crazy? But I did make the mistake of handling some of that stuff before I covered it back up. It was sort of interesting—especially the dog."

"Dog?" Joel said. His uncle hadn't mentioned

any dog when he'd told the tale before, nor had Joel found any dog bones in the grave. Of course, he hadn't uncovered all the skeleton. "You mean a dog was buried with the Indian?"

John Henry nodded. "It was right there against that Indian's side, like it was guarding 'im. It sorta got to me."

"Tell about the foot," said Lucy.

"Yeah, that was sorta pitiful. The Indian had about half his right foot missing. I covered 'em up—the Indian and the dog—just before that storm moved in."

Lucy shook her head. "That storm near about washed us away."

"And you think the Indian haint caused that?" Tom asked.

"I sure do!" John Henry replied. "That haint put a curse on me." His voice dropped. "Or maybe the dog did."

Joel swallowed. "Then what about those men coming in here and doing all that digging? Why ain't nothing bad happening to them?"

John Henry put down his fork. "Who says it ain't? Besides, far as I know, they ain't found nothing but arrowheads so far."

Joel hadn't thought of that.

"Let me tell you boys something," said John Henry. "You don't rob graves without paying for it. Especially Indian graves."

"What did you do to get rid of the curse?" asked Tom in a croaky voice.

"Only thing I *could* do," said John Henry. "I went down to the river, and I apologized right there beside that grave." He shook his head. "You don't mess with Indian graves."

By the time the boys went to bed, the wind was shrieking around the house and the peach tree outside the window was clawing at the panes. When the howling came, it was louder than ever. So was that other sound. It was like a heartbeat.

Finally, Joel could stand it no longer. He nudged Tom. "Is that a drum?" he whispered.

"A drum?" said his cousin, rolling over. "All I hear is the wind."

Joel heard more. He wrapped his head in his pillow, but still he heard it. Fear gripped his chest like a giant hand. Why had he dug up that grave? In his heart, he knew it was something he shouldn't do. He knew it as clearly as Tom had known it, but he had done it anyway. And now he had to pay.

"I'm sorry," he whispered into his pillow. "I'll take everything back tomorrow."

But it was no good. The storm continued.

At last he could stand it no more. "I know what I gotta do," he said, and scrambled from the bed just as a blast of wind hit the house with such force that the bed shuddered.

"Joel?" Tom said sleepily. "What are you doing? Where are you going?"

Joel found his overalls in the darkness and jerked them on. "I've gotta give back that Indian jewelry."

"Tonight?" Tom whispered. "Can't it wait till daylight?"

Thunder rumbled and lightning lit up the room. Joel glanced toward the window, and in that split second he saw something that sent a knife of terror through him. An Indian. He was limping along just beyond the trees, but he was coming steadily closer. Beside him was a dog.

"I can't wait," Joel cried, hurrying from the room. "I gotta get that stuff back in the grave, and I gotta do it tonight!"

"Joel!" Tom called, jumping out of bed and running after him to the back door. He grabbed Joel by the arm. "You'll get struck by lightning."

Joel broke free and lifted the latch. Driven by the wind and the rain, the door crashed against the wall.

Without looking back, Joel threw himself out into the storm and headed down the road toward the river. Only when the lightning came could he really see where he was. In between flashes, he kept to the road by memory and by feeling the bushes when he strayed too far right or left. He fell a number of times, only to jump up and run on.

Even as he ran, Joel heard the drumbeat. It grew steadily louder. He dared not look back when lightning lit the sky, but he felt the Indian and the dog behind him. When the howls came, they had a new intensity.

It was an eternity before Joel reached the mailbox. The blackberry briars ripped him as he waded in and flailed about, searching for the bag. At last he had it in his grasp and began stumbling downhill toward the river. He heard water roaring and churning before he could see it. Then several brilliant flashes of lightning revealed the river in all its fury. It was over its banks and licking at the very places where he'd dug that afternoon. Each spot was clearly marked by a pool of water, but at any moment the water might sweep in and cover everything. At any moment, it would be too late.

Groaning, Joel raced on. Finding the place by touch more than sight, he threw himself to his knees and clawed at the mud and water until his fingers touched bones. Frantically, he felt in the sack until he found what he knew was the disk. Then he found the armbands and beads and put them back, too, somehow knowing where each went.

"I'm sorry!" he screamed into the wind and rain with each piece he returned to the grave. But the lightning continued to flash, and the drumbeat grew steadily louder.

"All your things are back," Joel screamed, desperately trying to rake enough mud over the bones to cover them. "Everything's back just the way it was!"

Now he could go. But when the lightning flashed yet again, he saw the Indian and the dog. They were coming. They were coming for him. There was nowhere to go—nowhere to hide.

Then Joel looked to the right and felt a faint glimmer of hope. If he could run along the bank...if he could reach the bluff...if he could get the Indian and the dog between him and the river...if...

Turning, he sprinted toward the bluff. His only chance was to go around the Indian and his dog. But it was no good. The faster he ran, the faster the Indian and the dog moved. Each time the lightning flashed, Joel could see that they were nearer to him.

Reaching a tree by the bluff, Joel grabbed for it. Behind him and far below, he heard the river swirling and churning as though reaching for him. The *thud-thud-thud* of the drumbeat vibrated louder and louder, until it was louder

than the storm—louder than the dog's howls.

"I'm sorry," Joel screamed, knowing as he did so that it was no good. The Indian and the dog were coming for him.

Finally, he saw the Indian extend his hand.

"No!" Joel cried, shrinking back against the very edge of the bluff. He clung to a branch of the pine with both hands.

Suddenly the earth gave way beneath his feet. The tree was plummeting with him down into the angry water. Then it was ripped from his hands, and Joel clutched for something, anything, to save himself and found nothing.

The water took him. He felt himself being sucked down, down, down. He scrambled to fight his way to the surface, but the river would not turn him loose. It knocked him against something hard and turned him over and over.

When his lungs felt ready to explode, Joel broke through the surface long enough to gulp in a deep breath of air.

"I'm sorry!" he managed to whisper, and then the water sucked him under again. Struggling with every bit of strength, Joel tried to fight the power of the river, tried to get to the surface. He made it—but just long enough for one breath. He was going to drown. He knew that now. He would die in the river.

Then something was in the water with him.

He felt something butt against him. He felt something brush his arm, first on one side and then on the other. Then something took hold of his shirt, pulling him, and he had no strength to fight it. He was beyond caring. Blackness overtook him.

It seemed like a long time later when Joel woke to find himself on the riverbank. Day was breaking, and somewhere in the distance someone was calling his name.

"Tom," he murmured, and sat up. Then he looked at the muddy clay around him and saw two sets of footprints: One set belonged to a dog, and the other prints were those of a person—someone with only half a foot on the right side.

"Boy!" said one of the cousins near Mike's elbow. "If I ever run into a spirit, I hope it's a good one like that Indian haint."

"I don't want to meet up with any ghosts, myself," said Ernie, and Mike silently agreed.

"Maybe that haint saved Joel because he recognized one of his own," suggested their cousin John Ed. "A lot of folks around here have some Indian blood."

"My mother's mother was a full-blooded Cherokee," said Grandma.

"That means I'm part Indian too," said Mike in surprise.

"I don't think having Indian blood had a thing in the world to do with it," Grandpa said, returning to the story. "From what I hear, some haints are bad and others are good. I guess the Gusler family would know about that. They had a haint that mostly went about doing good."

There was a few moments' silence, and then Aunt Ruth asked, "Gusler?"

"Surely you've heard of the Guslers. That black family that used to live over beyond Macedonia Baptist Church."

"The ones that set such a store on schooling," Grandma said.

"The very ones," answered Grandpa. "Well, it was a Gusler haint that Ben Farabee ran into...."

THE CHOSEN ONE

Ben knew as soon as he woke that it was going to be a strange day. He knew it in his bones. It wasn't just that the farm was unnaturally quiet, with his two older brothers and the dogs still out on their all-night coon-hunting trip. It wasn't the weather, though the cold his father had been predicting seemed to be moving in. It wasn't even the heavy fog. It was something more.

"Tomorrow's hog-killing day," Ben's father said at breakfast, looking around the table at his wife, two daughters, and Ben.

Ben's heart sank when his mother added, "Reck-on Ben better go tell the Guslers we'll need help."

The Guslers. That meant he'd have to go by the Macedonia cemetery all by himself! He couldn't even take his dog. Over his protests, his brothers had taken Sam on their hunting trip.

"Why can't we get some other folks to help?" asked Ben, trying to keep the fear out of his voice. "The Deans're closer, and they'll work for part of the meat. The Guslers'll want money."

Dooley Farabee got up from the table and backed up to the kitchen stove, where his older daughter was stirring up the fire. "That's so, but the Guslers work a sight better," he said, and held out his coffee cup for his wife to refill.

"Ben's skeered of haints," said Ella Sue, the baby of the family. She moved over in front of him, shoelaces trailing as usual.

"I ain't skeered!" muttered Ben, squatting to tie his sister's shoes for the second time that day. How come a five-year-old knew him better than anyone else in the family? Of course he was afraid. Though he'd never been to the Gusler house, he'd heard all about the cemetery right next to their place.

Ben tarried as long as possible, hoping the fog would lift, hoping his brothers would get back with the dogs, hoping warm air would move in and put off hog killing.

None of those things happened, and at last he had to go.

"Why do I have to be the one to go to the Gusler place?" he asked when he was out of hearing, but he knew the answer. It was because he was always the one his family could spare. Unlike his four brothers and sisters, Ben was spindly. Worse, he was lame in one leg. At ten years of age, he was the errand boy.

Along the road, he passed places that would have been ordinary any other day. But today, with the fog, he seemed to be walking through a strange country. A strange country with dangers lurking everywhere. The chimney of the burned-out Owens place seemed to float in a cottony haze. Dark branches of tall oaks and green limbs of pines bobbed in and out of the mists. Once, just when he'd reached Macedonia Church Road, he thought he heard footsteps and hid in the ditch for a long time before hurrying on.

All too soon Ben rounded a steep curve that told him he was nearing the place he'd been dreading—Macedonia Baptist Church. His older brothers had scared him many times with hair-raising tales about this burying ground. Clyde and Matt both swore that if you went by the cemetery at night, a woman haint would come up out of the grave and take you back into the ground with her. But it didn't have to be night, Clyde had gone on to say. Sometimes spirits appeared in broad daylight.

"I ain't skeered of haints," Ben whispered.

He spotted graves through the trees off to his left. New ones were humped up with dirt. Older ones were flat, and the oldest of all were sunken in. Most of the stones were obviously home-cut, but a few were bought. Some had carved angels, lambs, or shepherds. One marker on the grave of a former railroad porter had a train on top. Ben's brothers claimed the haint from this grave came back with his train. "It whistles just like a real train," Matt had said.

"Dead people don't hurt you," Ben reminded himself. It was what he said to himself every time his brothers told stories about haints. And every time it did no good. It didn't help this time either. Neither did the fog. Fingers of mist were curling through the trees and snaking around the crooked tombstones.

Suddenly he stopped dead still. He caught a movement just this side of the church building. Then, with a flood of relief, he realized that it was one of the Gusler women. He had seen the Gusler women at Farley's store and sometimes at the Carter's Quarter post office. They were all cut from the same pattern. All of them had the same tall frame, wide shoulders, and dignified way of carrying their heads.

Ben heaved a big sigh. This would save him a heap of walking. He would tell her they needed help for the next day and then head back home.

Now unafraid, he cut off the road and hurried through the cemetery as fast as his lame leg would permit. The ground began to slope upward, and that made for even harder walking.

Ben figured that the woman had not yet seen him. She kept moving forward at a steady pace, stopping now and then at a stone marker. Probably reading them, thought Ben. That'd be like the Guslers—always reading something. None of the other families in Carter's Quarter went overboard on education. Like the Farabees, they got just enough schooling to read and write and do a little figuring. But the Guslers were a strange lot. They owned books—dozens of them, people claimed. They started their young'uns to school early and made them go until they finished the sixth grade. Now and again they'd send one off to college, and the whole Gusler family would hire out to pay school expenses. They used good money, that could've bought more land or built a better house, for schooling. It was plain foolishness, everyone said, but the Guslers didn't seem to know it.

Just then Ben spotted a glove on the ground. The woman must have lost it. He picked it up.

"Hey!" he called as the woman moved on again. "You dropped this."

The woman turned, pulling a thick shawl closer around her, and Ben could see her clearly. Her face was neither old nor young, but somewhere in between. Unwrinkled, it was like the rich polished mahogany of a new church piano. She wore her dress even longer than

Ben's mother and sisters did, but that too would be just like the Guslers. Many of their womenfolk never married. Several of them taught school off in other places.

"You dropped your glove," Ben told her, but the woman turned and walked on.

"Wait," he called. "Pa's killing hogs tomorrow and he wants two people to help. He'll pay cash."

The woman turned back and waited, staring at him as he limped toward her. Ben had long ago become accustomed to the stares of the curious, so he bore her inspection with indifference. He handed her the glove, and she bobbed her head once in acknowledgment. Then she motioned him to follow her.

"I've got to git back home," Ben said. She didn't answer, so he followed her uphill to the back edge of the cemetery.

She stopped at last in front of a large tombstone topped with a carved angel. The angel held a book and lifted one hand heavenward.

When Ben reached the grave, the woman pointed to the writing on the stone. What did she want him to do?

"Abigail," he read aloud after just a moment of studying. He read pretty well for someone who'd only been in school now and then over the past two years. "Abigail Gusler. Eighteen forty-one to eighteen eighty-nine. Is that your mother or something?" he asked to be mannerly.

The woman didn't answer. She pointed again, this time to the writing below the name and date.

Moss crusted part of the words, so Ben had to lean close to make out the letters. Slowly, he sounded out the words once and then a second time. "And gladly would he learn, and gladly teach." The words didn't have any meaning. He stood and found himself alone.

"Huh?" said Ben, swinging around quickly. He was the only person in the cemetery. Fog swirled in where the woman had been, and a low, moaning wind moved through the trees. The glove he had given the woman just minutes before lay on the grave now, one finger pointing toward Ben. A mournful train whistle echoed through the fog, and he recalled Matt's story about the ghost train.

Ben stumbled backward. Turning, he ran blindly through the fog. A strand of vine wrapped itself around his good leg and sent him sprawling into the sunken hollow of an un-marked grave. The ground seemed to give way beneath him, as though he was sinking into the grave.

Scrambling to his feet, Ben ran on, with bushes and tree limbs whipping and clawing at him on all sides. Each time he looked back, he thought he saw movement through the mists.

He came out of the woods at last, and relief washed over him. Ahead were the dim shapes of buildings. And there was a smell of cooking food in the air. He'd found the Guslers. He looked back one last time and then fell headlong into darkness. A star seemed to explode inside his head.

Ben woke in a dim room lit by a kerosene lamp. Black faces surrounded the bed where he lay. A woman leaned over him, holding a cloth and a pan. He closed his eyes again.

"He favor one of the Farabee children," a woman said.

"Mighty puny for one of them," a man said. "The Farabees are a sturdy bunch."

"Seem like I remember a crippled one."

"Yes, I forgot that one."

Ben blinked. "Am I dead?"

The woman with the cloth laughed softly, and Ben drew back at the sight of her face. She looked very much like the woman in the cemetery. "No, child," she said. "You fell in the old storm cellar. You got a smart-sized lump on your head."

"I'm Eli Gusler," said the only man in the group. "What is your business here?"

"I'm Ben Farabee," Ben said. "Pa sent me to git help with hog killing tomorrow." Ben touched the lump on his head. "I told the Gusler woman at the church. But she never answered." Now that Ben thought of it, the woman had not said one word.

"At the church?" Eli Gusler asked, looking around at the women. "None of our women been at the church today."

"I know what I seen," Ben said. "The woman looked just like her." He pointed to the woman who had just washed his face. "Only the one at the church was younger, and she was wearing a real long dress."

The women in the group drew in their breath sharply, and the man looked at Ben through narrowed eyes. Did they think he was lying?

Ben plowed on stubbornly. "The woman led me up the hill to the far side of the burying ground and commenced pointing to a tombstone." Then he recalled something else. "And it was a Gusler marker."

The man leaned closer. "What did the marker say, child?"

Ben closed his eyes, recalling the moss-encrusted stone, and haltingly spoke the words just as he had read them. "'Abigail Gusler. And gladly would he learn, and gladly teach.'"

The people pulled back. One of the women frowned and shook her head.

Ben pulled himself to a sitting position. "It don't make sense to me neither. But I know that woman was up there."

Eli Gusler looked at Ben for a long moment before speaking. "You're right, son," he said at last. "The woman was there. You met Abigail Gusler herself in that graveyard."

"Abigail?" Ben said, the stone flashing before his eyes. "But she's... She's..."

"Dead," said Eli, giving him the word he could not bring himself to say. "I know. She's been dead a long time."

"A haint!" cried Ben, falling back on the pillow. "I seen a haint?"

Nobody answered. While Ben tried to stop his head from spinning, the Guslers went to the far corner for a whispered conversation. Ben caught a few words every now and then, but none of it made any more sense than the

message on the tombstone. It seemed to him that Eli Gusler was on one side of whatever argument they were having and the women were on the other.

Ben wanted to escape. Easing off the bed, he moved toward the door, but he couldn't go—not until he had an answer for his father.

At last the Guslers turned back to Ben. The man looked at him solemnly. "You've been chosen," he said. "It's not for us to question— you've been chosen."

The circle of women didn't look too happy about it, but they finally nodded in agreement.

"Chosen?" Ben said. In spite of himself, the word felt good. Ben had never been picked for anything pleasant. All his life he'd been the one left out. The one who couldn't go hunting with Pa and the other boys because he'd only slow them down. The one who finished picking his row of cotton last. The one who couldn't be trusted to ride the mule. He'd resigned himself to always being the afflicted one. And now he was chosen? Doubt moved in and then suspicion. "Chosen for what?"

"To learn," answered the man. "And someday, to teach."

"Oh," said Ben, feeling let down. Chosen to keep going to school to listen to teachers like sour-faced Miss Pruitt and then to *be* a teacher like her? Cursed would be more like it, but of course he couldn't say that to the Guslers, who thought teaching was so wonderful. "I'm not smart enough," he said, and that was true too. His brothers reminded him often how slow-witted he was.

Eli Gusler shook his head. "Abigail wouldn't choose empty-headed people. And when she chooses you, she helps you," the man said.

Ben didn't think he wanted any help—especially from a haint. "I've had a bellyful of Miss Pruitt and stories about the little red hen that found some wheat." Because he was shy about reading aloud, Miss Pruitt never believed he was ready to move on to possibly more interesting readers. And maybe she was right; farm chores made him miss more days of school than he attended.

The man laughed. "You want to read about a boy your age going in a cave, finding buried treasure, and running off down the river with his friends?"

Ben stared at the man in disbelief. "Ain't no stories like that."

The man pulled a ratty-cornered book from the shelf and showed him. "The world got all kinds of books and all kinds of teachers. You'll be good. You've been chosen."

He hesitated a moment and looked at the women. Then he handed Ben the book. "It's yours."

Ben took it and reached for the doorknob. "Much obliged. I have to go," he said, throwing open the door. "Pa needs two people to help tomorrow. He'll pay cash. The usual amount, he said."

Eli Gusler nodded. "We'll come."

Ben stepped out into the yard. The cold wind that was blowing the fog away seemed to clear his head as well. He started out the road toward home, hardly noticing when he passed the church. It seemed to him that his world had suddenly become a bigger place. A place bigger than the Farabee farm. Bigger than Carter's Quarter. Bigger even than the state of Georgia. Maybe there was a place in that world for him.

By the time he reached his family's orchard, his shoulders were straight and his head high. His leg was stronger and his limp less bothersome. He heard the dogs barking and saw Ella Sue running to meet him at the edge of the yard.

"Ben?" she asked, staring at him.

Ben nodded, though he wasn't sure he was the same Ben who'd left home.

Ella Sue smiled. "Clyde said Sam was the best-trained dog, and Matt said he couldn't believe how much you learned him."

Ben nodded again. He *had* taught Sam. And he'd taught him without whipping him the way Clyde did his dogs. Ben tied Ella Sue's shoelaces and took her by the hand. "Come on, I'm going to teach you how to tie your shoes. And then maybe I'll read you some of this storybook I've got."

"Seems like I recollect the name Ben Farabee," said Aunt Ruth. "Wasn't he the one who was such a help to the army during the war?"

"Yes," said Grandpa. "He figured out all them secret enemy messages. Course, that was after he went to some big college up north."

"Sounds to me like he was smart," Mike ventured. "Figuring out secret messages and all that."

"No doubt about that," said Grandpa. "Ben Farabee was about the smartest person who ever lived in these parts."

"I wouldn't say that," Grandma replied. "There was Emily Lewis."

"Emily Lewis?" asked Cecil.

"Emily Renfro would be the name you'd know," said Grandpa. "She married Tate Renfro. Me and Emily went to school together. Her pa died when she was young, and then her ma died. She had it rough with the relatives that took her in. But I heard tell that she had a real good chance to get even one time...."

THE WISH QUILT

Emily Lewis raced through the woods, dodging limbs and underbrush. Behind her, she could hear her cousin Harry floundering through the autumn leaves, yelling her name. She wanted to scream at him to leave her alone, but that would only tell him where she was, and she wanted to get away from him and his family—at least for a while. None of them cared about her anyway. She was only an orphan relative they'd taken in to be a servant. Even today, when Uncle Gordon and Aunt Pearl were visiting relatives, Emily had to piece quilts with the women instead of playing with the other children.

Emily ran on. As the land began to slope

downward, she saw a large outcropping of rock off to her right. A place to hide! The rock was so big that she'd be able to edge around it from one crevice to another. Harry would never find her.

"Emily!" screamed her cousin moments later when he pounded into view. He was only a few yards away. "Maw says you better come back and finish that quilt top!"

"Tell Aunt Pearl I don't have to!" Emily whispered, pressing herself against the rock. "She always says my work is ugly." What she really meant was that Emily herself was ugly. She hinted about that often enough when she bragged about how beautiful her own daughter, Bess, was. Today she'd made it plainer.

"Dad'll be ready to leave soon!" Harry called.

"Leave without me!" Emily yelled. "I can walk home."

"You're going to get lost!" Harry bellowed. "You don't know these woods."

As if *he* did! The truth was, Harry didn't know the woods bordering Uncle Buck's farm any better than she did.

Rising on tiptoe, Emily watched Harry shrug and turn as she had known he soon would. He had no patience and didn't care any more for her than the rest did. When he staggered back over the hill the way he'd come, Emily jumped up and ran on. She wasn't going to ride home in the wagon with them. When she found the main road, she would walk. How she wished she could just keep going like her older brother, Lester.

Emily, Lester, and two younger brothers had been separated and taken in by different relatives after their widowed mother had died two years before. Last year the uncle who'd taken Lester had whipped him one time too many. At fifteen, Lester struck out for Texas. Emily had only gotten one scrawled note from him since. If only she could go join him! But she was only twelve years old and a girl, so she had to go back to her aunt Pearl and uncle Gordon Lewis. There was nowhere else to go.

"I hate them," Emily whispered, closing her eyes. The anger she felt rose up inside her and exploded in her head. "I hate them and I wish I could show 'em all."

A sudden quiet settled over the forest. The birds and squirrels hushed, and the air grew still and cold. The autumn sunshine dimmed, and there seemed to be a haze in the air. Even the crunch of the leaves under her feet sounded muffled, as if her ears were stuffed with cotton.

Emily reached the top of a hill and looked for a road. She didn't see one, but she did spot something else. Across a hollow and halfway up the next hill she saw a house. It was built of gray unpainted wood, and one end of the front porch was falling down.

There was something odd about the house, she decided. Then she realized what it was. It had no road leading to it, nor was there any cleared yard area around it. There were no outbuildings either—no barn, no chicken house, no well house. It was as if someone had picked the building up and set it down here only minutes before. Probably no one had lived in it for a long time, she decided. But wasn't that smoke coming from the chimney?

Emily headed toward the house. If someone lived there, she would ask directions. There must be a shortcut she could take—one that would allow her to get home without going back by Uncle Buck's house.

A woman appeared on the porch when Emily was still a good distance off. A beautiful woman. Someone she'd never expected to see in a dilapidated cabin in the mountains of north Georgia. Cats—a half dozen at least—clustered around the woman.

"You took your time," the woman said when Emily was a few yards from the porch.

Emily drew back. Had the woman mistaken her for someone else?

The woman tossed her head and laughed in a high, tinkling tone. Her hair was heavy, thick, and gleaming like the coat of a healthy animal. She waved a graceful hand, and the cats scattered. "I knew somebody was coming," she said. "I can generally tell."

"I'm Emily Lewis," Emily told her.

The woman nodded as if she knew that already. "I'm Catoma Blue. Come in, Emily Lewis."

Emily hung back. "I'm sort of lost. I need to know how to reach a road."

"All in good time," Catoma Blue said, and motioned toward the front door. "Come in and rest a spell first. You're just in time to eat a bite of cake with me."

Suddenly Emily was hungry. Aunt Effie's noon meal had been skimpy, even by her

standards, and had been eaten hours ago. Besides, Emily hadn't seen cake since the last church dinner.

Emily followed Catoma into a room that was larger than the entire house appeared on the outside. As her eyes adjusted to the dimness, she made out the usual furnishings—a table, cane-bottomed chairs, a cupboard, a bed, a washstand, and a trunk. There was a fireplace too, with a pot simmering among its coals.

But there were unusual things also—jars lined up in one corner containing twigs, leaves, and insects; dried plants on a wooden rack; a quilting frame of slick, dark wood; and strange pictures hanging on the wall.

While Catoma Blue punched up the fire and added something to the pot, Emily looked at the picture nearest her. It wasn't a picture at all, she realized. It was a small quilt made of tiny bits of fabric meeting at crazy angles. Then as she looked, the colors and patterns blended and swirled until she was dizzy. She blinked, and a picture began to form. A young woman and a young man were standing next to a river. They were happy and smiling.... No, the girl was almost crying and the boy was angry.... No, the girl was pulling away and the boy was reaching for her.... No,...

"Like it?" asked Catoma Blue as she set out

two steaming cups on the table beside two plates with cake.

"It's sad," Emily said, making herself turn away from the picture.

Catoma shrugged and motioned her to sit down at the table. "Depends on how you look at it."

The cake was like nothing Emily had ever tasted before. It was rich with fruits and nuts. The drink was sweet and spicy. She longed for another cup, but no more was offered.

"Let me see those scraps," Catoma Blue said when Emily pushed her cup and plate away.

"How did you know...," Emily began, dropping her eyes. Her quilting scraps were trailing from her pockets. It must have happened when she was running from Harry.

"These are for a quilt I was helping my aunt Pearl and aunt Effie with," she said. "I picked them for the colors."

She began to unload the scraps from her pockets and spread them for Catoma Blue's eager inspection. There was a piece of her last year's white muslin petticoat, a scrap of the pink printed voile that her mother gave her long ago, a snipping from her hand-me-down green wool coat from her cousin Bess. There was also a bit of her uncle Gordon's worn-out necktie, a scrap of blue ribbon from Aunt Pearl's best hat, and several pieces of blue chambray from her younger cousins' worn-out clothes.

"Ah, good," said Catoma Blue when each piece had been examined and identified. "Something from each member of the family."

Emily frowned. "Yes."

Catoma leaned closer. "You don't like your family?" Her voice was soft with understanding.

Emily felt tears stinging her eyes, but she blinked them back. "They're not my family. My mama and daddy are dead."

Catoma Blue nodded. Her eyes were large and sympathetic.

"I hate Uncle Gordon and Aunt Pearl and they hate me." Without planning to, Emily told her everything. How Aunt Pearl kept her up late at night to help with quilting, mending, and canning vegetables, yet complained constantly that she wasn't earning her keep. She told how she worked in Uncle Gordon's fields from spring planting until the last fall crops were in, yet he called her the worst farmhand he'd ever seen.

"When they let me go to school, I have to wear these old brogans because Uncle Gordon only buys shoes that last. So they make fun of me at school." She took a deep breath before telling the most hurtful thing of all. "And a while ago, I heard Aunt Pearl tell Aunt Effie that with my big feet and plain face they'd likely have me to feed forever."

Catoma made sympathetic sounds while the words hung there for a moment, as awful as when her aunt had said them. Then the woman turned, lifted the lid of the trunk, and pulled out a pair of scissors. "We're going to cut quilt pieces."

"No, thank you," Emily said, standing. "I've had enough of quilting for one day, and I've got to go."

Catoma Blue smiled. "This is different. We're going to make a picture," she said.

"A picture?" Emily said, looking quickly toward the young man and woman on the wall. Now both figures seemed to be looking at her and waiting.

"Yes," said Catoma Blue, looking straight at her. "And it will give you everything you want."

Emily laughed. "It can't do that. What I want is to be beautiful and smart. I want my uncle and aunt to be sorry for everything they've ever done to me."

Catoma Blue handed her the scissors. "Cut the patterns while I do a few chores."

Emily sat down. "How will I know which pattern goes with which fabric?"

"It will come to you," the woman said. And it did. The scissors seemed to slip through the fabric with a will of their own, and when all the fabric was cut, Emily began to arrange them without waiting to be told. She laid the pieces edge to edge. Somehow she knew where each piece should go, and soon she saw herself in the center of the picture she was making. She was beautiful—more beautiful than she ever dreamed she could be.

Girls began to take shape around that beautiful image of herself—girls from school. And she could tell just from looking at them that they envied and admired the Emily in the picture. They would never poke fun at *her*!

Cousin Bess began to form off to the right, and Emily was delighted to see that she was no longer pretty. Her face was crooked, and her hair was dull and thin. Uncle Gordon took shape, too. Far in the background, he was plowing what Emily somehow knew was someone else's land and doing it with a mule that looked ready to fall over dead.

"But he almost has his land paid for," Emily whispered, feeling a moment of pity. Then she shrugged. This was only make-believe. She looked back to the center of the picture and was less satisfied with her image this time. She rearranged fabric bits and added voile until the Emily in the picture pleased her once more. She smiled for a moment, but then she glimpsed the three girls surrounding her image. They didn't like the Emily in the picture, she suddenly realized. They feared her and they envied her—but they didn't like her.

"Who cares?" she whispered spitefully. They were only jealous. Returning to the background, Emily recognized her aunt Pearl taking shape. She was much older, and her clothes were more ragged than anything Emily had ever seen her wear. Her shoulders were stooped. Emily felt good about that. Let her see how it felt to be ugly!

But the good feeling lasted only a moment. She couldn't let Aunt Pearl look like that, she decided. Aunt Pearl was her mother's sister. She reached to take some of the voile from her own dress. Then she hesitated. It would ruin her dress to take any away.

Emily looked at her image again and caught her breath. The Emily in the picture was looking at her, and there was the beginning of a smile on her lips. The eyes were hard and mean. This Emily wasn't a good person. No wonder those girls didn't like her. Surely this wasn't how she made her. Surely this wasn't how she herself was.

The thought was like a blast of cold wind. Emily's head cleared, and suddenly she knew. She *was* this girl. Or she was going to be. She looked at Catoma Blue. "Is this me?" she asked.

The woman looked back at her, but she said nothing.

Afraid, Emily jumped up from the table. "I'm not this way. I'm not mean and selfish like this girl. I'm not."

Emily backed toward the door, but the cats barred her escape. They seemed to have grown. They were now much larger than any cat she had ever seen. Their fangs were showing, and their fur was raised.

Emily looked back at Catoma Blue. "That's just a picture, and I'm not going to be like that girl."

"You don't want to be beautiful?" Catoma asked, moving toward her.

Emily hesitated. She *did* want to be beautiful. She wanted to wear pretty clothes and have friends. But she didn't want them this way. She didn't want people to fear her. She didn't want to hurt anyone.

Catoma Blue moved closer. "You don't want everyone envying you?" she asked in a low and silvery voice.

Emily fought down the temptation to give in. "Not if I have to be like she is," she said, pointing to the picture on the table. "I want to be..." She hesitated. What did she want? "I want to be whatever I am."

Catoma Blue's smile was cold. "It's a little too late for that now."

Emily glimpsed herself in a wavery mirror

over a washstand and gasped. She looked exactly like her image in the picture! "No," Emily cried. "It's not too late. I won't be like that."

In one quick move, she leaped toward the table and swept the fabric bits together into a wad.

"Stop!" Catoma Blue shrieked, grabbing at her, but Emily dodged and threw the fabric on top of the logs in the fireplace. Flames exploded and the cabin blazed with light as sparks flew out into the room. Before Emily swung around and headed for the door, she had one brief glimpse of Catoma Blue as a horrifyingly ugly woman.

Forcing her way through the cats, Emily leaped off the porch and raced downhill. She could hear the woman calling her name and the cats hissing right behind her. But she didn't look back. She reached the bottom of the hill, splashed through a narrow stream, and tore up the hill on the other side. Only when Emily reached the top did she look back. The house with the crooked porch was gone.

🌙

"Sounds like Catoma Blue's cats turned into painters in the end!" said Cecil, laughing.

"Could be," Grandpa said. "I warn't there."

"Painters?" said Mike.

"City folks may call 'em panthers or mountain lions, but they'll always be painters to me," answered Grandpa Nolan. "A painter's a fearsome beast. It's half as big as a cow. It screams like a woman, and it can cut you to pieces with its claws."

Mike drew closer to his grandfather's rocker. "Are there any living around here now?"

"I ain't seen any lately. But some people swear they hear 'em back in the mountains between here and Ludville."

Grandma put her hand on Mike's shoulder. "Don't worry none, child. Some men'll swear to anything."

Grandpa grunted. "Tell that to Calvin Oats. I warn't there the evening he met that painter over at the Weems place. And let me tell you, I'm glad I warn't. Calvin Oats was never the same again...."

THE PAINTER

Calvin Oats hated Octavia Farley. He'd hated the skinny girl ever since she'd gone to work in her brother's general store. There was a time when he'd been the center of attention whenever he stopped by the store on his way home from school. Back then, he'd buy himself a cold drink, prop up his feet by the potbellied stove if it was winter or near the front door if it was summer, and just wait for an audience to gather. And they would.

"Tell us about that snake you seen with two heads," one of the young'uns would say. Or "Tell us about that funeral where the preacher fell in the casket with the corpse." Sometimes even a grown-up would listen to his stories, though he was only fourteen.

Calvin would take a swig of his drink and act like he was thinking real hard. Sometimes he'd hold out until every last young'un in the store was waiting for him to speak. Then he'd begin.

Now hardly anybody asked. Not since Octavia Farley moved back from Alabama to help her brother in the store. Octavia couldn't have been any older than Calvin, but she had already quit school and acted like she was grown. She'd marched right in with her stories of haints and murders and people possessed and stole the show. These days, if Calvin ever got to tell a story, somebody was sure to say, "That puts me in mind of that story Octavia told last week. How'd that go, Octavia?"

Octavia was always happy to oblige. "Well, it was long about dark," she'd say in her sharp, whiny voice. Near about every one of her yarns used that line. For the life of him, Calvin couldn't figure why anybody listened to her. But all Calvin's classmates acted like she was the best storyteller that ever was.

Yes, he hated Octavia, Calvin decided as he swung along the highway that sunny autumn afternoon. To tell the truth, he didn't like the store that much anymore, either. He'd told himself every day this week that he wouldn't stop off there anymore. But habit was strong. Besides, if he got home too early, Maw and Dad would be on him to chop stovewood or fix the front doorstep. Since the older young'uns left home, they tried to work him to death.

He came in sight of the store and smiled. Along with several wagons, two cars, and a truck, there were two old school buses used to haul cotton pickers. The store would be full of customers, so Octavia would likely be busy clerking. Calvin hurried to the store.

His smile faded when he stepped through the doorway. Octavia was behind the cash register, all right, but all the young people were circled around her. "...It was just getting good dark," she was saying.

Calvin grunted. "Naturally."

"Sh-h-h-h!" several boys hissed.

"She's telling about a painter," one of the Moss boys said.

Calvin laughed. He had her now. People who tried to top Calvin's yarns always told stories about panthers. "They ain't no painters around," he said. "Ain't been any living here since my grandpa was a boy."

Octavia's eyes flickered in Calvin's direction for a moment, and he lost some of his confidence. Her eyes were a strange gold-green.

They almost glowed. "I ain't claiming this one was *living*," she said.

The Moss boy drew in his breath sharply. "A ghost painter?"

Octavia shrugged. "I wasn't there. This painter would only come at night. And you know how dark it can get in the woods around the Weems place."

There were mumbles of agreement. In spite of himself, Calvin felt prickles on his neck. There had been rumors from time to time about panthers back in those hills and hollows around the Weems place. The dark and twisted trees in that area always made Calvin feel uneasy. It wasn't just the crooked tombstones scattered here and there among them or the rock with the outline of a human skull worked into its colors. It wasn't even the Indian cave that sometimes gave out strange moaning noises. It was how he felt there—like something cold and frightening was sneaking up behind him.

Octavia went on. "They could hear that painter coming closer and closer, traveling through the treetops." She leaned over the counter. Her eyes had become a true green now, and they glowed more than ever. "They went in the house and closed it up tight. Even closed the shutters. Then that painter commenced screaming. Newt Weems said it sounded just like a woman."

"Probably *was* a woman," said Calvin, shaking off the chill. "Them Weems women are *loud*." This brought a chuckle from several people.

Octavia tossed her limp brown hair until her red hair ribbon danced. "There they were, in that house with no gun, and that painter coming after 'em."

"With *his* gun," Calvin said, and felt a mean satisfaction when a titter rippled around the group. He was ruining her story.

"Then a wind whipped through the house," Octavia said, her voice dropping low. Her audience leaned forward. "The windows rattled and the floor creaked. Slowly the lamps went out one by one and the house was dark as pitch. They couldn't find the matches nowhere—"

"So they just used old man Weems's nose," broke in Calvin. The whole crowd laughed. Everyone knew about Newt Weems's now-and-then drinking sprees.

Octavia glared at Calvin, her eyes like green slits. Calvin wanted to avert his eyes but couldn't.

At last she turned back to the group. "That's when they heard something clawing its way up the side of the house." Her skinny hands made climbing motions. This was the first time Calvin had noticed her hands. They were long and bony, and the nails were sharp. He followed those hands and could see that panther climbing the side of the Weems house, pulling itself to the rooftop....

Calvin again felt the chill on his neck. He couldn't help remembering his father saying that Newt Weems's hair had turned white almost overnight. He shook off the thought as Octavia continued.

"Newt heard footsteps on the shingles," she whispered. "The footsteps went round and round that roof and then walked right up to the chimney..."

"I need a smoke," said Calvin in a high-pitched voice.

When the laughter died down, Octavia turned on Calvin. "I take it you don't put stock in painters."

Calvin tore himself away from her eyes and glanced around the group. "Sure, way back yonder," he said, hoping nobody would remember that painter story *he'd* told a while back. "But the only people that see 'em these days is scaredy females that don't get out in the woods."

Octavia smiled, but her eyes glinted hard as steel. "Then I reckon you wouldn't mind delivering a few things to Newt Weems."

Calvin drew back. "Today?" He glanced outside. The sun was getting low.

Still smiling, Octavia nodded. "On your way home," she said, smooth as honey. Quickly she reached under the counter and pulled out a box containing sugar, coffee, and tobacco.

She'd set a trap for him! She'd had that box waiting for him all along. She'd intended for him to mock her, intended him to go to the Weems place.

"I'd like to oblige," Calvin began, licking his lips, "but..."

"Unless you're scared of that painter," Octavia said, dragging out the words.

"It ain't that," Calvin said, and glanced around the group. Some of the onlookers were smiling; a few were smirking. Two of his class-mates nudged each other.

Trembling with anger, Calvin snatched the box from Octavia's hands and headed for the front door.

He cussed her all the way to the place where Beulah Church Road turned off Highway 411. By that time, he was cussing himself for stopping at the store today, for allowing Octavia to trap him, for coming on this fool errand.

He stopped. "Why don't I just set this box down in the bushes and light out for home," he said. Then he groaned. If he did that, he'd never hear the end of it. No doubt Octavia Farley would check to see if the box was delivered. And she'd make sure everybody else knew it hadn't been. He'd never be able to face the boys at school.

He was trapped. He had to deliver that box— or Octavia won again.

The sun was down when he saw the fallen-down shell of Beulah Church. One ragged wall of the building was still standing, outlined dark against the reddened western sky. The chimney was like an accusing finger. The Weems road was just ahead.

"I ain't afraid," Calvin whispered when he turned onto the narrow road. "I ain't afraid of no painter."

But he couldn't help seeing the twisted tree that looked like a person—a person lifting bony

arms and long fingers. Its hollowed trunk gaped in a silent scream. And beyond that were the ghostly tombstones, each with a sunken hollow in front of it.

Calvin ran. He passed the rock with the skull and then the cave.

He had just caught a glimpse of Newt Weems's house when he heard the cry of a hawk. Calvin stopped dead still. It was a sign. A bad sign. A hawk didn't cry this near dark except for one reason. Somebody was about to die.

"I won't be here when it happens," he muttered, and raced on toward the house. He reached the overgrown yard moments later. "Mr. Weems!" he yelled, plunking the box down in the shadows of the sagging porch. "Miz Weems! I brought your stuff from the store!"

His words echoed in the silence. The door remained closed. Then he noticed the shutters. They were closed tight—every one of them. The house seemed empty.

A wind stirred, and from somewhere behind the house came a soft, padding rustle, followed by a scratching, climbing sound. A climbing sound?

Calvin put a hand to his throat and stumbled backward, eyes raised to the roof. Then, swinging around, he raced away from the house and up the road.

He was just passing the skull rock when he heard a scream. It was like the scream of a woman, and it ripped through the twilight like a knife.

"The painter!" Calvin said. He knew it was, even though he had never heard one scream before.

He turned to look over his shoulder and fell sprawling in the dirt. He blinked. There in front of his nose was a red hair ribbon.

A picture of Octavia's hair flashed across his mind. He jumped up, shaking his head. That scream—it was exactly the way he knew Octavia Farley would scream. Her slanted, glowing eyes came back to him with all their fire. Those eyes didn't just look at you—they burned clear through you. And those hands. He remembered the nails. No, claws! That's what they were.

"Octavia Farley can't be the painter," he said, shaking his head again. That was witch stuff. He didn't believe in witch stuff.

The scream came again. The panther was following him! Calvin put on more speed, tearing past the twisted tree and onto Beulah Church Road. If only the church had still been standing, he might have taken refuge there until daylight. There were no other buildings on the road, no places to hide.

The highway! If he could make it to the

highway, he might escape. There would be passing cars and trucks—he could flag down one of them! Could a painter outrun a car? "I'll roll up the windows!" he said out loud.

The panther screamed once again, but this time it was close enough for him to hear it leaping through the trees, clawing its way from branch to branch. It would leap on his back! It would claw him to pieces.

Then, through the tunnel of dark trees ahead, Calvin saw a passing flash and almost sobbed. The highway! He was nearly there!

At last the pavement was right in front of him, and he could see a truck rounding the curve off to his right. "Stop!" he yelled, running to the center of the road and waving his arms. "Help!"

The truck stopped with a screech of brakes, and Calvin tore around to the passenger side and threw open the door. The driver said, "Calvin Oats? Something wrong?"

Calvin fell into the truck, slammed the door, and checked the window. He fell back against the seat. Safe! Safe!

The man leaned toward him. "You okay, Calvin?"

It was Willie Hill, their closest neighbor. Had he been at the store earlier? "The Weems place—," Calvin began, then stopped and looked toward Beulah Road. Nothing. There was no painter.

He took a deep breath and tried to speak in a normal voice. "Just hurrying home to cut wood for Maw," he said, taking in a gulp of air. "Could you give me a lift?"

The man looked puzzled. Then he smiled. "You trying to scare me with one of your ghost yarns?" he said, and pulled the truck back onto the highway.

Just as the truck began to pick up speed, Calvin glanced back at the dirt road. This time he saw something—a girl. A skinny girl standing in the shadow of a twisted tree.

"Was Octavia Farley a witch?" asked Ernie, taking the question right out of Mike's thoughts.

"No," said Grandma. "All this business about witches and spells is foolishness. There ain't no such thing as a witch."

There were a few moments of silence, and then Aunt Dorrie cleared her throat. "I can't speak for Octavia Farley," she said. "I never did know her. But I knew Myra Tippet, and a heap of folks thought she was a witch. Hannah Logan was sure of it...."

CTHE NECKLACE J

Hannah walked beside her dog, Brownie, swinging her bucket of blackberries. She listened while the other kids in the crowd argued over how much to charge for their morning picking.

"How about twenty-five cents a quart," said Leon Craig, setting down one of his buckets to claw at his waist. "With all the chiggers and scratches, it's worth every penny of that."

There was a chorus of agreement from the others. Then Betty Grey spoke up. "Yeah, it's worth it, but nobody's going to pay that."

"Especially not tightwad Myra Tippet," Hannah said, pushing Brownie's nose away from her bucket with her leg. "You know how she is.

She never pays more than half our price. And year before last she didn't pay us anything."

"Then we'll skip her and go on to the next house," said Leon.

"We can't," Hannah replied. "She sent word she wanted berries. My mama'll skin me if I don't go."

"Mine too," Betty said. "She's always talking about how bad Miz Tippet's had it this year, with her cow dying, her barn burning, and that bad fall she had."

"And then she lost her boarders when the sawmill moved on," Hannah added.

"Far as I'm concerned, it couldn't happen to a person who deserved it more," said Leon.

Everyone agreed, but in the end they went to the Tippet house anyway. Myra Tippet was sitting on the front porch snapping beans when they arrived. Hannah ordered Brownie to lie down out next to the road. Miz Tippet hated dogs.

"Stay with Brownie and I'll give you a nickel," Hannah told the youngest Craig girl. "Don't let him in the yard and don't let him chase a car if one comes along." Chasing cars was Brownie's one bad habit.

"Well, well, what do we have here?" Myra said, as if she didn't know. "My goodness, blackberries!" Her eyes glittered. "I guess the price is cheap, with them being so plentiful this year."

"Twenty-five cents a quart," said Leon.

"Twenty-five cents! Are these made of gold?"

"We're saving for a ball and bat so we can play baseball," said Hannah, hoping to soften the woman. She took a tobacco sack from her pocket and shook it. "We have about half what we need in here."

Myra Tippet's eyes narrowed at the sound of the change rattling. Then she inspected the buckets. "Well, I tell you what, I'll empty these into a dishpan and inspect 'em; then we'll talk price."

"You want all of 'em?" said Hannah. "Among the ten of us we have eighteen quarts."

"Eighteen skimpy quarts, maybe," said Myra Tippet. "I'll measure 'em after I inspect 'em. While I'm doing that, you young'uns can do a few chores for me and stay out of mischief. You boys go out to the garden to gather the rest of my green beans." She turned to the girls. "My flower beds need weeding, and I need somebody to draw me some water from the well."

Hannah volunteered to draw the water, thinking Miz Tippet only wanted one bucket. But as Hannah headed toward the well house, Myra called, "I need four or five buckets. I'll want plenty to wash berries and beans. And don't let that mutt of yours come in my yard."

"He's not a mutt," Hannah whispered fiercely. She decided to take her time.

It was while she was slowly turning the well windlass that something glittering on one of the well house posts caught her eye. It was a gold chain that had been flung carelessly over a nail. On the end of it was a teardrop-shaped pendant with a red stone.

"A ruby?" Hannah whispered. That was her birthstone. All her life she had wanted a birthstone ring like a couple of the popular girls in school wore. Of course, she knew it was out of the question and had never asked for one. And

here, apparently tossed aside unwanted, was a necklace. That was even better than a ring!

She brushed her fingers over the necklace as she passed the post. When she returned to draw the second bucket of water, she lifted it off the nail for a moment.

As soon as Hannah touched the necklace, something happened to her. It felt good in her hand. Suddenly she wanted the necklace more than she'd ever wanted anything in her life. And why shouldn't I have it, she thought, recalling every bad thing Myra Tippet had ever done to her and her friends.

She never pays us enough for our blackberries, Hannah thought. And she always makes me work for nothing when I pass by on the way to Grandma's house.

On her last trip to the well, Hannah looked around quickly and then put the necklace around her neck. She dropped the pendant down inside her dress and felt the weight of it. Although she had told herself she would only try it on, from the moment she put it around her neck, she knew she would not take it off.

When the chores were finished, Myra Tippet handed them their empty buckets. She was all smiles now. "I'm going to pay you for eighteen quarts, even though they were skimpy ones. But I figure fifteen cents each is a gracious plenty, especially when you've tracked up my porch and kitchen the way you have." She counted out two dollars and fifty cents in change and grinned while Hannah dropped the coins into the tobacco pouch. Then she waved them on their way.

"Come on, Brownie," Hannah called as they left the yard. "Let's get out of here."

Leon grunted in disgust when they were well away from the Tippet house. "Two dollars and fifty cents. That ain't fifteen cents a quart! She shorted us."

"I know," Hannah answered, and felt a mean gladness for taking the necklace.

The good feeling didn't last long. Hannah caught and ripped her dress when she was climbing through the barbed wire fence to take a shortcut through the Tippet pasture. It was her second-best dress, and her mother had told her not to wear it berry picking. A few minutes later, she fell off the log crossing the creek.

"Looks like that Tippet bad luck's rubbed off on you," said Leon when Hannah pulled herself out of the stream and climbed up the creek bank. "Better check your cow when you get home." Everyone laughed, and Hannah made herself laugh along with them.

It wasn't until the kids went their separate ways and Hannah was by herself that she began to examine the thing she'd done. She had stolen something. She had stolen something she couldn't even enjoy. She was going to have to hide the necklace. But with five younger brothers and sisters and two older ones, there was no place in their crowded house to hide anything.

Hannah took out the pendant and examined it in the sunlight. It didn't look as beautiful as it had back at the well.

"Where will I wear it?" she whispered. At school her brothers and sisters would see it. And if they didn't, her classmates would talk about it, and word would get back to her mother. She couldn't wear it to church, and she couldn't even wear it when she went to visit her best friend, Lena.

Hannah was still deep in thought when she neared the road. Otherwise, she would've heard the car coming in time to grab Brownie. But she didn't hear, and Brownie was off like a bullet.

There was no stopping him once he was on the chase, but she tried. Screaming "Stop! No!" she ran after him. But he was out of sight before she reached the road. She heard a thud and a high-pitched yelp as she scrambled down the road bank. Looking left, she saw a dark form through a cloud of red dust.

"Brownie!" she screamed, though she knew it was too late for him to hear even before she reached his still form. She cried for a long time before she pulled him into the ditch. She would have to get her oldest brother to help her bury him.

"It's my fault," she said, recalling Leon's words about the Tippet luck. Suddenly she knew he was right. She had taken Myra Tippet's necklace, and now she was being punished.

Hannah pulled the necklace off and looked at it. It was ugly to her now. Why had she ever wanted it? She didn't want to wear it anymore. Taking the tobacco pouch from her pocket, she dropped the necklace inside with the money.

"I'll return it," Hannah whispered, heading back the way she came. Maybe she could go to the well house without Myra Tippet even seeing her. She would hang the necklace exactly where she'd found it.

The Tippet house was quiet. Hannah saw smoke coming out of the chimney and thought she smelled cooking blackberries. Myra Tippet must be canning.

She took the tobacco pouch from her pocket and tiptoed toward the well house from the back. But as she rounded the corner, Myra Tippet stepped out.

"You can just head on back home, young lady," she said.

"I...I..." Startled, Hannah retreated several steps and then stopped. She had to do what she'd come for. "I took..."

"I know what you took," the old woman said. "And you can't give it back. Can't throw it away either. I tried that. It won't let you. You took it, and now it's yours. You better just hope it don't kill you before somebody steals it from you."

"You mean the only way I can get rid of the necklace is to let somebody else take it?"

Myra Tippet laughed. "Not *let* 'em take it, honey. Make it *easy* for 'em to take it would be more like it. Do everything but *beg* 'em to take it—along with all the bad luck that goes with it."

Myra's eyes dropped to the tobacco pouch in Hannah's hand. "You and them other young'uns damaged my bean plants and messed up my flower bed. I'll just take this for damages," she said, scooping up the sack.

"But...," Hannah said, and paused. "That's stealing."

"Call it what you will," said Myra Tippet. "But you messed up my garden and my flowers and you're paying. Now get out of here."

Hannah turned and ran. She was halfway across the pasture when she heard Myra Tippet scream.

"Hannah Logan made her own bad luck by taking something that wasn't hers," said Grandma. "And Myra Tippet done the same thing for herself when she stole the necklace back. There was never any curse or magic about it."

"Could be you're right," Grandpa said.

"And I tell you something else I got right too," Grandma continued. "It's way past bedtime. These young'uns need to turn in."

Mike was beginning to agree. Both Ernie and Kate had fallen asleep during the last story. Kate was using his right leg for a pillow, and Ernie was snoring softly.

"One more story, and then we'll call it a night," Grandpa said. "This'un is about someone you know, Ora—Lessie Hendrix."

"Lessie Hendrix?" said Grandma.

"Lessie Daniels, she was, back when you made her acquaintance. Course, you didn't meet her until long after the Danielses lived next to that hainted house just south of here...."

THE GIRL IN THE PAINTING

It was a pleasant April day, though there was a little bite in the wind. All along the road through Carter's Quarter, Lessie Daniels smelled the good scent of newly turned soil. Lots of farmers were doing exactly what her father was doing on the tenant farm they'd just moved to—planting. In fact, that was the reason for Lessie's trip. Her father had decided he would need another pound of cottonseed to finish out his twenty acres.

Lessie saw Harve Dennis long before she reached Farley's general store. He was standing outside with several other boys, smoking. She'd only attended the new school a few days, but she already knew to stay out of

Harve's way. He was a bully and a troublemaker.

"Stay close to me, Wilma," she whispered to her little sister, "and don't talk to anybody."

It was the wrong thing to say. Wilma pushed out her bottom lip. "I'm gonna ask if anybody's seen Bootsie."

"Forget about that cat," Lessie answered. "I told you it ran off because we moved to a new place. That's the way cats are."

Harve stepped forward. "Hey," he said. "Ain't you some of that ignorant Daniels family from Gordon County that moved into the old Thorn house a few days ago?"

"No," Lessie answered without slowing her pace. Harve scared her, but she wasn't going to let him know it. "We're some of the *smart* family that moved *next* to the Thorn house."

There was a ripple of laughter from the other boys, but Harve glared them into silence. "Same difference. That place is hainted."

Lessie shrugged and walked around Harve. "Ain't you too big to believe in ghosts?"

Wilma broke free of Lessie's hold. "Have you seen my cat?" she asked Harve. "Bootsie is yellow with three white feet and—"

"What'd I tell you?" Harve said to the other boys. "That's the first sign. The haint has already got their cat."

Wilma broke into tears, and Lessie's fear of

the boy was swallowed up by anger. She walked back to face him. "Don't you have anything better to do than scare little kids?"

Harve put on an innocent look. "Hey, I'm trying to do you a favor. Ask anybody around here. Ask 'em what happens to everybody that tries to live there. There's a haint in that house." He lowered his voice. "It's a little girl, but she's real mean. She plays the piano. Go look for yourself. There's a painting of her inside. But if I was you, I wouldn't git too close to it. It's hainted too."

Wilma's eyes were large. "Did the haint get Bootsie?"

"I'd put money on it," Harve answered. "You been hearing any music? The haint plays music when she's trying to get you."

Lessie grabbed Wilma's hand and dragged her toward the store. "Come on, Wilma. We're not afraid of ghosts. After we buy Daddy's seed, we might just go over to the Thorn house and look for your cat."

When they came out of the store, Harve and his buddies were gone. Lessie breathed a sigh of relief and shifted the bag of cottonseed to her other arm. Now all she had to do was make Wilma see reason. "I only said we might go to the Thorn house to aggravate Harve, but I didn't mean it," she explained. "Harve is a liar. He just wanted to scare you. Besides, we need to get this seed to Daddy."

But no matter how many times she explained things, Wilma refused to change her mind. Finally, Lessie was the one who gave in.

"But if Daddy finds out, I'm going to blame you," Lessie warned, even though she knew that was an empty threat. Since Lessie was eleven and the oldest, she'd be the one her father would scold. Jim Daniels had told all four of his children to stay away from the deserted house. "Part of the reason I got a good deal on this place is because the Thorns trusted me not to go prowling around the old homeplace," he'd said.

"We'll just go and take a quick look so you can be satisfied," Lessie told Wilma as she turned off the road to take a shortcut through the woods. "If you can't find Bootsie, then you shut up about her from now on. Okay?"

Reluctantly, Wilma nodded.

They approached the house from the back. It was just as big and lonely looking close up as when they saw it from the tenant house across the pasture. And the long shadows of late afternoon didn't help either.

Lessie was uneasy. Maybe it was the fact that the long-unoccupied house still had curtains at some of the windows, and here and there she could see a piece of furniture. There were two rockers on the back porch and a water bucket next to the door. It was almost as if someone still lived here.

Lessie wanted to walk on tiptoe and speak in whispers. But she couldn't let Wilma detect her fear, so she walked briskly and made herself speak in her normal voice. "All right," she said to Wilma, "we're going to walk around the house one time. You call Bootsie all you want to. Then we're going home."

Wilma broke loose from her clutches and ran on ahead, calling between cupped hands, "Kitty-kitty. Here, kitty-kitty. Here, Bootsie!"

"Watch where you're stepping," Lessie called. "Snakes could be out, or there could be broken glass."

She could have saved her breath. Ignoring weeds and briars and whatever they hid, Wilma kept running. She stopped every now and then to peek in the shrubbery or underneath the house.

Glimpsing a movement in the corner of her eye, Lessie swung around to look at the tall window nearest her. Nothing was there. Then she saw that the shutters hung loose on either side of the window. Probably one of them had shifted a little in the breeze.

"Dang Harve Dennis!" she muttered. She was

playing his game, letting his dumb stories scare her. Hurriedly she moved on. Wilma was already in front of the house, still calling "Kitty-kitty."

At the front porch, Lessie paused at the sight of tracks on the steps. Cat prints? She was glad Wilma had missed them.

Lessie moved closer, her eyes following the tracks up the steps and across the porch to the front door. The door was closed, and there were no tracks coming back down. Whatever went in hadn't come out—at least not by this door. But that didn't mean anything. No telling how long those tracks had been there.

"Wilma!" she yelled, and ran on around the house. Wilma was already out of sight. "Wilma, wait for me!"

Halfway around the side of the house, Lessie heard something inside the building. It was sort of a soft hissing sound—like the sound a scared cat makes. She looked up at the window, but she was a bit too short to see inside. The sound came again. Could it be Bootsie?

Suddenly she recalled Harve's comments about the cat, and a whole new idea came to her. Harve lived only a couple of miles away. It would've been easy for him to lure the cat inside and close it up in there. It was the kind of rotten thing he'd do.

Looking around, Lessie spotted some bricks

outlining a weed-infested flower bed. Just what she needed. Putting down the cottonseed, she hurriedly gathered bricks and stacked them until they were high enough. Then she stepped on them and peered through the dirty glass. For a moment she saw nothing. But as her eyes adjusted to the dimness, she made out a cluttered room with water-stained wallpaper. There was an upright piano against one wall.

Then in a corner she saw a large painting. It wasn't hanging on the wall the way one would expect but was standing on the floor. It was a painting of a little girl about eight years old. She wore an old-fashioned pink dress with a white lace collar. The girl was looking directly at Lessie, and there was a smirk on her otherwise pretty face. Then Lessie saw what the girl was holding under one arm and gasped. A *cat*. A yellow cat with three white paws.

She jerked backward, and the bricks shifted beneath her feet. Lessie tumbled into the weeds. Leaping up, she ran for the backyard.

"Wilma!" she yelled. "Wilma, come here right now!"

She found her sister on the back porch, trying to open the door. "Bootsie's in there," Wilma said.

"No, she's not," Lessie said, gathering the little girl up in her arms. "Let's go."

"No," Wilma wailed. "I want to get Bootsie."

"She's not here," Lessie said, heading for home by the quickest route. She no longer cared if her parents caught her coming from the forbidden Thorn house. She no longer cared about anything but getting away from that place.

Only when she was halfway across the pasture did Lessie set Wilma down. "Don't ever go there again," she told her. "Not ever. That's a bad place. Besides, you promised me. You said if I took you and let you look, you'd hush up about that cat."

Wilma pushed out her lower lip and wiped her eyes with the back of her arm. As Lessie started on once more, she heard something. The sound of a piano playing very softly. Determined to ignore it, Lessie held Wilma's hand tightly and walked on.

Suddenly she stopped. "The seeds," she whispered. "I left Daddy's seeds next to the window." She looked toward home. She had bought those seeds on credit. Her family needed the money they would get from the cotton those seeds would grow. She groaned. She had no choice. She couldn't go home without the seeds. She would have to go back.

Lessie looked toward the Thorn house. The red-orange sun, slanting low through the crooked trees, was reflected in a crazy broken

Lessie swung around to find Wilma. "What are you doing here?" Lessie demanded, her heart pounding. "Didn't I tell you to wait..."

Before she could finish, Wilma stepped inside and started down the hallway. "Stop!" Lessie whispered, throwing down the seed and hurrying after her.

Just then the music stopped, and wild screams blended with the unmistakable yowling of a cat. A split second later, a group of boys filled the doorway, punching and fighting to get out first. Finally, out in the hall, they knocked Wilma down and galloped past in a blur of faded blue overalls and chambray shirts. Lessie had a fleeting glimpse of pink, too, before the boys

pattern from the windowpanes. And she could still hear the music.

"You wait here," she told Wilma. "I've got to go back and get the seeds."

The music grew louder and louder as she neared the house. By the time she reached the yard, the trees seemed to dance in time to it. She tried not to hear, tried to keep her mind only on what she'd come for.

Darting around the far side of the house, Lessie hurried to the pile of bricks and scrambled about in the grass until she found the bag of seed. Jumping up, she started back around the house. The music was still playing, only now she thought she heard voices too. And every now and then there were hissing sounds, meowing, and low sniggering.

When Lessie reached the front steps, she saw that the door of the house was open. Slowly she moved closer. She crept up the steps one at a time. At the doorway the voices were louder, but she still couldn't make out what they were saying.

She took a quick peek. There were closed doors down both sides of the hallway, but on the left next to a stairway was an open door. It had to be the room with the painting, she decided.

"They've got Bootsie, don't they?" said a voice behind her.

were out the front door and gone. But there was no time for her to think about it. Wilma was scrambling up and heading for the room the boys had left.

"Stop!" Lessie screamed, racing for the doorway. She arrived just in time to catch a wild-eyed cat.

"Bootsie!" said Wilma.

The cat was hissing and clawing, but somehow Lessie managed to hold on to it until Wilma could tear off her sweater and wrap it around the animal.

Only when they started out of the room did Lessie look back and see the painting. She blinked. It had changed. The girl and the cat were gone. Now there was a boy of thirteen or fourteen in the painting. His eyes were large with terror, and his hands were raised as if pressing against a glass wall. It was Harve Dennis.

☾

"I still don't put no stock in that crazy story of Lessie's," Grandma said, getting up from her rocker.

"Didn't you hear the piano playing that time Lessie took you by the old Thorn house?" Grandpa asked.

Grandma hesitated. "Yes, but it was way back

yonder. Anyhow, that don't mean a thing. Somebody was pulling a trick."

"Maybe so, but then again..."

"Well, either way, the house is gone now," said Grandma, pushing her rocker up against the wall.

Cecil took the hint. "Time to go home," he announced. "Young'uns, load up."

Moments later truck engines roared to life.

Mike helped Ernie and Kate into the house. His grandmother lit a kerosene lamp and led the way to the back bedroom, where the three of them would sleep.

Soon the house was quiet except for the snores of the two old people in the front bedroom. Outside, the night was as dark as ever. The crickets and the frogs had almost lulled Mike into sleep when he heard something else, faint and far away.

It was the sound of a piano playing.